Know About
Charles Dickens

MAPLE KIDS

KNOW ABOUT CHARLES DICKENS

Published by

MAPLE PRESS PRIVATE LIMITED
office: A-63, Sector 58, Noida 201301, U.P., India
phone: +91 120 455 3581, 455 3583
email: info@maplepress.co.in
website: www.maplepress.co.in

Reprinted in 2019

ISBN: 978-93-50335-78-9

Contents

Preface

Charles Dickens was the most prominent writer in the English language during the nineteenth century. To this day and age, he remains one of the best selling and most important authors of all time. Although stiffly Victorian in appearance, Charles Dickens had a lot to say and chronicle in his massive body of work, which includes fifteen novels and five novellas among others. His writing held a mirror to the many dreadful things in Britain at that time: rampant corruption, crime, poverty and an absolute lack of human empathy.

During his literary career, he came across as a restless, poetic wanderer, mixing observation, autobiography and fables in his remarkable works. Most of his works portray his talent for acute observation and creativity. In addition, they give a panoramic window to the novelist's attitudes and pre-occupations.

Employed early in life, Charles Dickens' novels give us an insight into his childhood experiences. He used these very experiences to lure people in the troubles of the poor and downtrodden in society and make them emotionally interested. Charles Dickens was the most prolific writer of his times, a genius, who has continued to inspire artists of every generation through his works.

Chapter 1
Charles Dickens is Born

Charles Dickens was born to Elizabeth Dickens and John Dickens, the second of eight children, on the 7th of February 1812, at Landport in Portsea Island (Portsmouth). John Dickens was a clerk in the Navy Pay Office. In January 1815, he was transferred back to London, and the family moved to Norfolk Street, Fitzrovia. When Charles was four, the family moved again, this time to Sheerness, and then to Chatham, Kent, where he stayed until the age of 11. His early years seemed to be pleasant and happy, though, in his writing, Charles describes himself as a small and somewhat neglected boy.

Charles spent considerable time outdoors, but also read voraciously, including the novels of Tobias Smollett and Henry Fielding, as well as *Robinson Crusoe* and *Gil Blas*. Charles' interest in literature might have also been triggered by his father's small collection of books. The books were kept in a little room upstairs, which led out of Charles's own. *Roderick Random, Peregrine Pickle, Humphry Clinker, Tom Jones, The Vicar of Wakefield*, and

Don Quixote would engross him entirely in the world of stirring narratives. This little attic provided him with the literary education that shaped the entire course of his life. His writing was marked by incidents that often seemed to be inspired by his own life; Dickens' vivid memories of his childhood and a brilliant memory helped make his books realistic. His father's years as a clerk in the Navy Pay Office helped him gain some years of private education, first at a dame school, and then at a school run by William Giles, in Chatham.

Later in life, he recalled that his first desire for knowledge and his earliest passion for reading were awakened by his mother, from whom he learnt the basics of not only English but also, a little later, of Latin.

Living much beyond his means, John Dickens was soon forced by his creditors into the Marshalsea debtors' prison in Southwark, London in 1824. His wife and children soon joined him there. Charles, then 12 years old, stayed up with Elizabeth Roylance, an impoverished old lady and a family friend, at 112 College Place, Camden Town. She was the inspiration for "Mrs Pipchin" in *Dombey and Son*.

The school-boy Charles was a handsome, curly-headed lad, full of animated spirits. He was connected with every mischievous prank in the school. On one occasion, he led his friends to Drummond-Street and the group started pretending to be poor boys. They asked the passersby for charity. Dickens' main targets were the old ladies. With his trusting face, he would persistently demand money from them. Some of the old ladies would shove him away by saying that they had no money for beggar boys. On such adventures, Dickens would surprise the old ladies by the rudeness of the demand and then, would explode with laughter and take to his heels.

For the teachers at school, Charles was a responsive, attentive and a headstrong boy. This feeble-bodied little boy was popular among his teachers and peers, for the knowledge of literature that he had gained at home. The teachers were amazed to see the unusual imagination and the wandering intelligence he possessed. His mind could be easily turned to good or evil, happiness or misery, by a mere play of words. Consequently, he secured the status of one of the preferred students of Mr Giles. Seeing Charles' commitment to acquire knowledge, he pronounced him a boy of capacity.

Before the Dickens family left for the Somerset House, Mr William Giles gave Charles a Goldsmith's Bee as a keepsake. In Camden Town, Charles felt as if he had left all the joy and happiness in his life behind in Chatham. All his dreams and ambitions were about to meet with cruel realities. He was to enter a school far severe than that in Clover Lane.

The Dickens' new house had a miserable little back garden adjacent to a dirty court. In the sudden solitude that engulfed him, he would remember the days, when he enjoyed the company of the boys of his own age. A Gray's Inn solicitor, with whom Charles's father, John, had had dealings, was attracted by the bright, clever look of Charles and took him as a clerk in his office. Once again, Charles was employed for work.

This time, he started off with a modest salary of thirteen and sixpence a week. Later on, it was raised to fifteen shillings a week. He remained in Mr Blackmore's office from May 1827 to November 1828, but he had lost none of his eager thirst for distinction. He planned to spend his entire spare time mastering Gurney's shorthand and reading at the British Museum.

Several incidents took place in the office, which Charles observed keenly. Some of those incidents found a place in his *Pickwick* and *Nickleby*. His father had become a newspaper parliamentary reporter to support family resources. Charles continued to live with him. He took a sudden determination to qualify himself thoroughly for what his father had become.

The quality that marked Charles different from other lads was that whatever he tried to do in life, he tried with all his heart to do well. What he devoted himself to, he devoted himself completely. He never allowed any failure to affect his work. These became the golden rules, which ruled his life and work.

Chapter 2

Dickens' Early Years in Journalism

Now 20, Dickens felt energetic and immensely creative. Though he indulged in the art of mimicry and popular entertainment, he was directionless as to what he actually wanted to become, and yet he knew he wanted fame above anything else. Always attracted to the theatre, he landed an acting audition at Covent Garden, where George Bartley, the manager and the actor, Charles Kemble were to see him. He decided to impress them with a caricature of Charles Mathews, but he missed the audition because of sickness.

He soon set out to be a writer. His first story, "A Dinner at Poplar Walk", came out in 1833, in the London periodical, *Monthly Magazine*. One of his uncles, William Barrow, offered him a job in *The Mirror of Parliament* and he worked in the House of Commons for the first time in early 1832. He wrote for and edited journals throughout his career. George Hogarth, the *Chronicle*'s music critic, launched an evening edition for the *Morning Chronicle* in January 1835. Hogarth invited Dickens to contribute *Street*

Sketches to the paper. He soon became a regular visitor and enjoyed the company of Hogarth's three daughters—Georgina, Mary, and nineteen-year-old Catherine.

In November 1836, Dickens accepted the position of editor at *Bentley's Miscellany*, where he worked for three years until he had an argument with the owner. In 1836 he finished the last instalments of *The Pickwick Papers* and began writing *Oliver Twist*—writing as many as 90 pages a month. He also wrote four plays and oversaw their production. *Oliver Twist*, published in 1838, became one of Dickens's most famous and loved novels. It was the first Victorian novel with a child protagonist.

Chapter 3
Dickens as a Fledgling Reporter

Charles' love of conversation helped him to create vibrant characters in his stories. He followed a strict routine when it came to his writing. He woke up at a fixed time and went to sleep at another. He would write for hours between breakfast and lunch.

Dickens' flair for writing soon made him one of the most sought-after journalists in London. He firmly held the opinion that those men who had later on assumed important roles and ranks in London society started off as journalists reporting on the various debates in the Parliament. When he was 19, in 1831, he entered the gallery of the House of Commons as a reporter for the *True Sun*. Later, he worked as a reporter for the *Mirror of Parliament* and then for the *Morning Chronicle*. Dickens occupied the top ranks in the House of Commons, right among its eighty or ninety reporters. Not only was his reportage accurate, but also he excelled at transcribing. Though polite and well-mannered, Dickens was a quiet young man. He kept to himself and did his work and was known for his reserved nature.

Meanwhile, John Dickens was still a frequent visitor to the sponging houses. In a letter to his school friend, Tom Mitton, Dickens mentioned the arrest of his father at a wine firm and begged Tom to go over to Cursitor Street and try to settle the matter. Tormented by the sufferings and downfall his father's actions brought about, Dickens nevertheless held the care and love his father had for him, in high regard.

Chapter 4

Charles Visits the United States

Dickens and his wife sailed aboard the RMS *Britannia* and arrived at Boston, Massachusetts on the 22nd of January, 1842. The Dickens household was joined by Georgina Hogarth, Catherine's sister who came over to look after the young family they had left behind. She stayed with them

for many years, till Dickens' death, acting as housekeeper, caregiver and governess. Dickens modelled the gentle character of Agnes Wickfield after Georgina.

Dickens chronicled his vivid impressions and experiences in the States, in a travelogue called *American Notes for General Circulation*. In *Notes*, Dickens vocally criticized slavery which he had also written about in *The Pickwick Papers*.

Dickens returned to Washington, D.C. from a trip to Richmond, Virginia, and made way to St. Louis, Missouri. He wished to see an American prairie before he went back home. A group of 13 men travelled with Dickens to the Looking Glass Prairie, 30 miles into the state of Illinois.

During his visit to America, Dickens spent a month in New York City, giving lectures, and speaking about copyright laws.

Chapter 5

Back in London

In 1845, Dickens was again back in London. He continued enjoying his favourite hobby of private theatricals. In January 1846, he was briefly the editor of a London morning paper, the *Daily News*. By early spring he was back at Lausanne. There, he wrote his customary letters to his friends. The letters spoke of how he missed his London streets. He also started working on *Dombey and Son*. In the midst of writing letters, he made it a point not to miss his fourteen-mile walk, which he had daily. Dickens sent his new work to Eton and began saving money. Artistically, it was less satisfactory; as it contained some of Dickens' prime curios, such as Cuttle, Bunsby, Toots, Bliniber, Pipchin, Mrs MacStinger and young Biler. A long rest at Broadstairs followed this period.

After that, Dickens returned to the native home of his genius. With the start of 1849, he began to prepare for *David Copperfield*. The book *David Copperfield* (1849-50) contains Dickens' his own personal experiences of work in a factory. David's widowed mother marries the

"*Familiar in their Mouths as* HOUSEHOLD WORDS."—Shakespeare.

HOUSEHOLD WORDS.

A Weekly Journal.

CONDUCTED BY

CHARLES DICKENS.

VOLUME II.

FROM SEPTEMBER 28 TO MARCH 22.

LONDON:
OFFICE, 16, WELLINGTON STREET NORTH.
1851.

tyrannical Mr Murdstone. David becomes friends with Mr Micawber and his family. In the later part of the novel, Dora, David's first wife, dies and he marries Agnes. He pursues his career as a journalist and later as a novelist.

"Of all my books," Dickens wrote, "I like this the best;

like many fond parents I have my favourite child and his name is David Copperfield."

The book is peppered with scenes of early boyhood in the book, by the picture of Mr Creakie's school, the Peggottys, the inimitable Mr Micawber, Betsy Trotwood and that monument of selfish misery, Mrs Gummidge.

A new two-penny weekly called *Household Words* began circulation by the end of March 1850. Dickens used them to form a direct means of communication between himself and his readers. The weekly was a means of collecting material around him and encouraging the talents of the younger generation. No one was better qualified than him for this work. Whether it was his complete freedom from literary jealousy or his magical gift of inspiring young authors, he did the work with his same old style that successfully made people admire him once again.

Chapter 6
Charles Dickens the Philanthropist

The heir to the Coutts banking fortune, Angela Burdett Coutts, approached Dickens in May 1846 and talked to him about setting up a home as a shelter for working-class women. She wanted a safe haven for these women and

give them a safe environment, one in which they could learn new things and have some education. Not ready to go ahead with the idea initially, Dickens finally gave in and founded the home, named "Urania Cottage", in Lime Grove, Shepherds Bush. He looked after and managed this home for women for ten years.

During this period, whilst thinking over a project to give public readings to earn money, Dickens was approached by the Great Ormond Street Hospital, to help it survive its first major financial crisis. His essay, '*Drooping Buds*' appeared in *Household Words* on 3 April 1852. It was considered by the hospital's founders to have been the catalyst for the hospital's success.

Dickens, whose generosity was well-known, was asked by his friend, Charles West, the hospital's founder, to take the chair over the appeal, and he threw himself into the task, compassionately. Dickens's public readings earned sufficient money for a contribution to be made to the hospital's cause. The hospital was now on a sound financial footing—one reading on 9 February 1858 alone brought in £3,000.

Chapter 7

A New Collaboration

Dickens' popularity ceased as nothing helpful came from the *Monthly*. However, even before the February number of the magazine appeared, Dickens had found a new place to show his writings. A countryman, Mr George Hogarth was responsible for its preparation. Dickens was communicating from his rooms in Furnival's Inn.

Hogarth played a major part in bringing a good turn in Dickens' life. He allowed Dickens to form certain hopes and fancies. This was the beginning of his knowledge of an accomplished and kindly man. Gradually, his relations with Hogarth's family became so intimate that they had an influence on his entire future career. Mr Hogarth had asked him, as a favour to himself, to write an original sketch for the first number of the enterprise. In writing back to say with what readiness he should comply and how anxiously he desired to do his best for the person, who had made the request, he mentioned what had arisen in his mind.

Dickens begged to ask Mr Hogarth whether it was possible if he commenced a regular series of articles under some attractive title for the *Evening Chronicle*. He considered that its conductors would think he wanted to have some additional remuneration for doing so. He made it clear that he expected a little money for the sketches. Further, if they were satisfied with the first proposal, he wanted to know, whether they would allow him to continue the ordinary reporting business of the *Chronicle*. This ensured him an added financial advantage. He would receive something for the papers beyond his ordinary salary as a reporter.

Dickens' request was thought fair. He began the sketches and his salary was raised from five to seven guineas a week.

Throughout the year, Dickens delivered sketches with great spirit and freshness. Dickens and his editor would often talk of things outside as well as in the world of newspapers. However, nothing in connection with them delighted the writer half so much as the hearty praise of his own editor, Mr John Black. Dickens to the last remembered that it was most of all the cordial help of this good old mirth-loving man, which had started him joyfully on his career of letters.

Chapter 8

Start as an Author

An interesting anecdote of Charles reporting days tells us about the sharpness he followed in his work. Mr Stanley had, on an important occasion, made a speech. All the reporters found it necessary to abridge it. *Morning Chronicle* listed the essential points of his speech very well. Impressed by this, Mr Stanley sent a request to the reporter to meet him in Carlton House Terrace and take down the entire speech. Dickens attended the request and did the work accordingly. His work was much to Mr Stanley's satisfaction. Years later, Dickens was

THE

VICAR of WAKEFIELD

A TALE

By OLIVER GOLDSMITH.

Illustrated by George Thomas.

London:
SAMPSON LOW, SON AND CO. 47 LUDGATE HILL.
1861.

A DINNER AT POPLAR WALK

BY

CHARLES DICKENS

BEING HIS FIRST EFFUSION, "IN ALL THE GLORY OF PRINT."

REPRODUCED IN FACSIMILE FROM
THE MONTHLY MAGAZINE
DECEMBER, 1833.

invited as a guest of the Prime Minister in the same room in which Dickens took the speech.

In the meanwhile, however, he had started as an author in a more creative sense. He started penning some sketches of contemporary London life. Those sketches were like the ones he had attempted in his school days in imitation of the sketches published in the London and other magazines of that day. The first of these appeared in the December number of the *Monthly Magazine* in the year 1833.

Since the first sketch appeared in the *Monthly Magazine,* nine others appeared in the same magazine, the last of which came in February 1835. Another of his sketches, which appeared in the preceding August, had the first signs of 'Boz'. This was the nickname of a pet child, his youngest brother Augustus, who in honour of the *Vicar of Wakefield* was dubbed Moses. The word, if jokily pronounced through the nose became 'Boses'. Dickens shortened the word and called it Boz. Thus, he had fully invented his sketches by 'Boz'. The sketches appeared before they were even so-called, or anyone was ready to give much attention to them. The magazine was owned, as well as, conducted at that time by Mr Holland.

Chapter 9

Dickens' Religious Views

As a young man, Dickens expressed dislike for certain aspects of religion. In a pamphlet in 1836, he opposed a plan to prohibit games on Sundays in defence of the people's right to pleasure.

Dickens respected the figure of Christ—though some sources say otherwise. His son, Henry Fielding Dickens, claimed Dickens had deeply religious views. He also wrote a religious book, *The Life of Our Lord* in 1846, a short book about the life of Jesus Christ, written to share his faith with his children and family.

Leo Tolstoy and Fyodor Dostoyevsky referred to Dickens as a great Christian writer.

Chapter 10
The Middle Years

In December 1845, Dickens became the editor of the *Daily News*, a newspaper daily based in London, a paper through which Dickens hoped to promote, in his own words, progress, improvement, education and civil rights, religious liberty and equal rights among others. Among the other contributors, Dickens chose to write for the paper was the economist Thomas Hodgskin and the social reformer Douglas William Jerrold. Dickens barely worked there for ten weeks, before he voluntarily resigned, frustrated and tired of frequent arguments with one of the paper's co-owners.

The Dickens, who loved the French, often spent time vacationing and holidaying in France. In a speech delivered in Paris in 1846, in French, Dickens called the French "the first people in the universe." On his visit to Paris, Dickens met motley of the brilliant French writers, Alexandre Dumas, Victor Hugo, Eugène Scribe, Théophile Gautier, François-René de Chateaubriand and Eugène Sue.

In early 1849, Dickens started to write *David Copperfield* which was published between 1849 and 1850. In *Life of Charles Dickens* (1872), Dickens' biography, John Forster wrote of how *David Copperfield* was autobiographical in parts- many incidents in it had happened in Dickens' life as well. It happened to be Dickens's personal favourite

among his own novels, which he mentioned in the author's preface to the 1867 edition of the novel.

Dickens wrote *Bleak House* (1852–53), *Hard Times* (1854), and *Little Dorrit* (1856) in Tavistock House, where he had moved into, in late November 1851. It was here that he participated in the amateur theatricals mentioned in Forster's *Life*. During this period he was on very intimate working terms with the novelist and playwright Wilkie Collins. The royalties he earned from his writing allowed him to buy Gad's Hill Place in Higham, Kent in 1856. As a child, Dickens had always dreamed of living in it.

In 1857, Dickens decided to hire professional actresses for the play *The Frozen Deep*, written by him and Wilkie Collins. Dickens fell in love with Ellen Ternan, one of the actresses, and this love affair would last for the rest of his life. Dickens was 45 and Ternan, 18 when he decided to separate from his wife, Catherine, in 1858-at a time when divorce was still taboo and against conventional Victorian standards. Catherine left, never to see her husband again, and she took with her, one child, leaving the other children to be raised by her sister Georgina who chose to stay at Gad's Hill.

After his separation from Catherine, Dickens undertook a series of immensely popular and reading tours that brought in lots of money. This together with his journalism took up almost all of his creative energies for the next ten years, in which he wrote only two more novels. His first reading tour, from April 1858 to February 1859, consisted of 129 appearances in 49 different towns throughout England, Scotland and Ireland. Dickens's constant fascination with the theatrical world was moulded into the theatre scenes in *Nicholas Nickleby*. He soon found an outlet in his public readings. In 1866, he undertook a series of public readings in England and Scotland, followed by more in the following year in England and Ireland.

Chapter 11

Working for Chapman and Hall

One of the chief vogues during that time was the issue of humorous, sporting or anecdotal novels in parts with plates. Ainsworth, Bulwer, Marryat, Maxwell, Egan, Hook and Surtees represented some of the best talents of the day. They had set the standards for acceptability and appreciation of work.

During that time, the publishers were not slow to perceive Dickens' aptitude for this species of 'letterpress.' A member of the firm of *Chapman Hall* called upon him at Furnival's Inn in December 1835. They proposed him to write about a Nimrod Club of amateur sportsmen. At the same time, the comic illustrations were to be etched by Seymour, a well-known rival of Cruikshank, who was the illustrator of Boz. The offer was too tempting for Dickens to lose, but he changed the idea from a club of Cockney sportsmen to that of a club of eccentric peripatetic. However, he did soon sensible grounds. He knew that the sporting sketches were stale. *Secondly*, he knew nothing worth speaking of about sport.

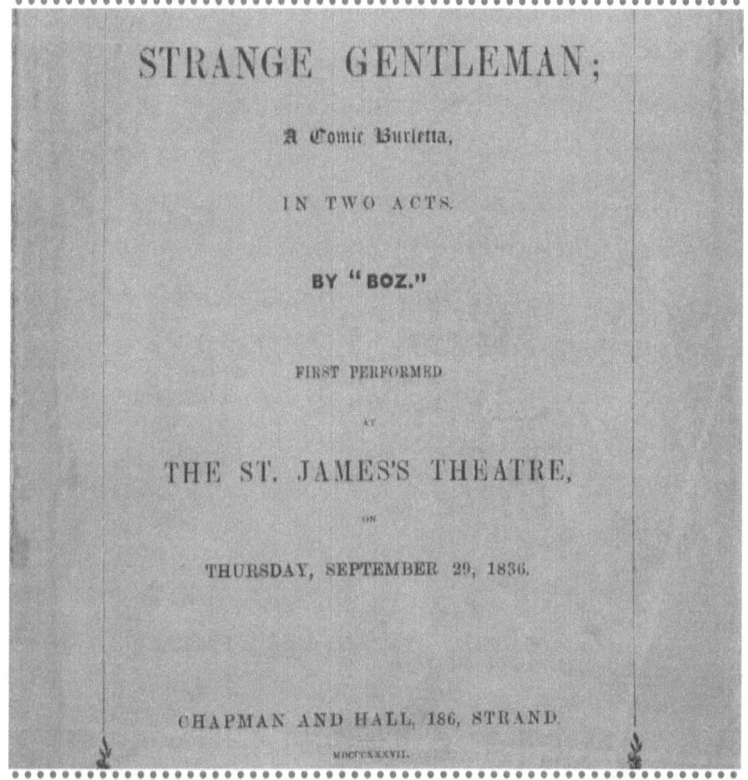

STRANGE GENTLEMAN;

A Comic Burletta,

IN TWO ACTS.

BY "BOZ."

FIRST PERFORMED

AT

THE ST. JAMES'S THEATRE,

ON

THURSDAY, SEPTEMBER 29, 1836.

CHAPMAN AND HALL, 186, STRAND.

MDCCXXXVII.

The first seven pictures appeared with the signature of Seymour and the letterpress of Dickens. Before the eighth picture appeared, Seymour had blown his brains out. After a brief interval of Buss, Dickens obtained the services of Hablot K. Browne, known to all as 'Phiz.' Author and illustrator were as well suited to one another. They joined hands for the common creation of a unique thing. Having got rid of the sporting element, Dickens found himself at once. He found the subject that exactly suited his knowledge was his skill in arranging incidents. He realized his limitations too.

The Session of 1836 terminated Dickens' connection with the gallery and some fruits of his increased leisure showed themselves before the close of the year. His eldest sister's musical attainments and connections introduced him to many cultivators and professors of that art. He was led to take much interest in Mr Braham's enterprise at the St. James's Theatre. In aid of it, he wrote a farce, founded upon one of his sketches. He also wrote the story and songs for an opera composed by his friend Mr Hullah. Both the *Strange Gentleman* acted in September and the *Village Coquettes,* produced in December 1836, had good success.

A few days before the marriage, just two months after the appearance of the Sketches, the first part of *The Posthumous Papers of the Pickwick Club* was announced. No modern book was so incalculable. It leads the reader on through a tangle of adventure, never allowing him to predict what is before him.

Chapter 12

Dickens and the Pickwick Club

The landscape changed for Dickens and the rest of the writers after the publication of *The Posthumous Papers of the Pickwick Club*. Pickwick became the symbol of kindheartedness, simplicity and innocent humour. Dickens struck a deeper note in the Fleet Prison. In the book, he writes about the medley of human relationships, the loneliness, the mystery and sadness of human destinies. He reveals the tragedy of human life amid its most farcical elements. The foolish and laughable figure of the hero was changed by the kindliness of human sympathy. It was now a kind and bespectacled angel in shorts and gaiters.

Dickens rose above the traditions by defying accepted rules. He had produced a book to be protected from then on in the hearts of all of his countrymen of all sorts and in all conditions. In addition, he definitely enlarged the boundaries of English humour and English fiction. As for Mr Pickwick, he is a fairy-like Puck or Santa Claus, while his creator is "the last of the mythologists and perhaps the greatest."

Dickens became immensely popular when *The Pickwick Papers* appeared in book form at the close of 1837. After the appearance of Sam Weller in part V, the universal hunger for the monthly parts rose to a furore. The book was, promptly translated into French and German. As a result, the author had received little assistance from the press or critics. He had no influential connections. In addition, his class of subjects exposes him at the start to accusations of vulgarity. The truth was hard to handle.

Yet, in less than six months from the appearance of the first number, as the quarterly review almost regretfully admitted, the whole reading world was talking about the Pickwickians.

The names of Winkle, Wardle, Weller, Jingle, Snodgrass, Dodson & Fogg, became as familiar as household names. *Pickwick* chintzes figured in the linen drapers' windows and *Pickwick* cigars in every tobacconist's. Weller corduroys became the stock-in-trade of every breeches-maker. Boz cabs were seen rattling through the streets and the portrait of the author of Pelham and Crichton was scraped down to make way for that of the new popular favourite on the omnibuses. A new and original genius had suddenly sprung up. There was no denying it, even though, as the quarterly concluded, "it required no gift of prophecy to foretell his fate—he has risen like a rocket and he will come down like the stick."

It would have needed a very definite gift of prediction indeed to foretell that Dickens' reputation would have kept on rising until the present day. Except for one sharp fall, which reached an extreme at about 1887, Dickens' popularity stands higher than it has ever stood before.

Chapter 13
Enjoying Public Fame

After accepting the respect of the greats of the literary, artistic and theatre worlds, as if it had been his natural due, he decided to settle with his family.

On January 6, 1837, Dickens' son was born. Before the close of the following month, he and his wife went to the lodgings at Chalk, which they had occupied after their marriage. In March, he went to 48, Doughty Street.

Meanwhile, the instalments of *Pickwick* were gaining popularity with every passing day. However, the celebration of the anniversary of the birth of Pickwick was preceded by a few weeks of personal sorrow, which profoundly moved him. His wife's youngest sister Mary, who lived with them, died suddenly. By the sweetness of her nature, she had made herself the ideal of his life. Her death completely bore him down. His grief and suffering were intense and affected him severely.

As a result, the publication of Pickwick was interrupted for two months. Charles was so overwhelmed by grief that

the effort of writing was not possible for him. He moved for a change of scene to Hampstead and came back within a few months.

Dickens went to the place with the popularity and fame that Pickwick brought for him. He spoke at innumerable banquets, public and private gatherings in the country, at the seaside, in France or in Italy. He sorted out in public almost every topic relating to political, ethical, artistic, social or literary issues. He entertained and legislated for an increasingly large domestic circle, both juvenile and adult. He started ruling himself and his timetable with a rod of iron.

The animation of Dickens' look was so that it attracted the attention of anyone, anywhere. His figure was not that of an Adonis, but his brightness made him the centre and pivot of every society he was in. The keenness and vivacity of his eye combined with his excessive appetite for life gave the unique quality of the style to all that he wrote.

Dickens' instrument is that of the direct, strong English of Smollett, combined with much of the humorous grace of Goldsmith. Smollett and Goldsmith were his two favourite authors. However, his text is modernized to a certain extent that it comes under the influence of Washington Irving, Sydney Smith, Jeffrey, Lamb and other writers of the London Magazine. He taught himself to speak French and Italian, but he could have read little in any language. His ideas are those of the undeveloped and narrow-minded liberalism of the thirties. With his unique force in literature, he was to owe to no supreme artistic or intellectual quality. The gift of language he had can be attributed, almost entirely, to his extravagant gift of observation, his sympathy with the humble, his power over the emotions and his incomparable endowment of unalloyed human fun.

Chapter 14

Another Great Work

While the people were still rejoicing in the first sprightly running of the 'New Humour', Dickens set to work desperately on the grim scenes of *Oliver Twist*. It is the story of a parish orphan. The nucleus of the novel had already seen the light in his *Sketches*. On August 22, 1836, Dickens signed an agreement with Mr Bentley to undertake the editorship of a monthly magazine. The magazine was to be started the following January.

Dickens was required to supply a serial story to the new magazine. Soon afterwards, he agreed with the same publisher to write two other tales. The expressed remuneration in each case was inadequate to the claims of a writer of any marked popularity. Under these Bentley agreements, he started writing, month by month, the first half of Oliver Twist.

The early scenes of the novel are of a disturbing reality. In spite of the germ of forced pathos, which the observant reader may detect in the pitiful parting between Oliver and little Dick, what struck every reader at once in this book was the directness and power of the English style. Nervous and unadorned from its unmistakable clearness and vigour, Dickens travelled in the novel, as far as time went on.

Oliver Twist contains the full effect of Dickens' old simplicity. However, the book found a circle of admirers, not so wide in its range as those of others of his books. The people, who appreciated the book, were of a character and mark that made their honest liking for it and steady advocacy of it. It proved important Dickens' fame. Ever since the story has held its ground in the first class of his writings. It deserves that place.

Before the end of November 1837, Charles Dickens entered on an engagement to write a successor to Pickwick on similar lines of publication. Oliver Twist was then in mid-career. A Life of Grimaldi and Barnaby Rudge were already covenanted for. Dickens forged ahead with the new tale of Nicholas Nickleby and was justified by the results. Its sale far surpassed even that of Pickwick. As a conception, it is one of his weakest. An unmistakably 18th-century character pervades it. Some of the vignettes are among the most piquant and besetting ever written. Large parts of it are totally unobserved conventional melodrama. But, the Portsmouth Theatre and Dotheboys Hall and Mrs Nickleby (based to some extent, it is thought, upon Miss. Bates in Emma, but also upon the author's Mamma) live forever as Dickens conceived them in the pages of

Nicholas Nickleby. Never before were characters so surely revealed by themselves, as they did in this new book. As a result, reality made itself felt at once. The characters talked so well that everybody took to repeating what they said. The sayings, which were the constituent elements of the characters, became part of the public.

Chapter 15
After Nicholas Nickleby

One kind spark of humour in *Nicholas Nickleby* is the good little miniature painter Miss La Creevy, who lived by herself. Dickens made her a character who overflowed with affection. In the book, Dickens portrays her as someone, who has no one for company but is always cheerful by way of good-heartedness. When she is disappointed in the character of a woman she has been to see, she eases her mind by saying a very cutting thing at her expense *in a soliloquy.* This illustrates the advantages of having lived alone so long, that the only confidante she had was herself. Due to that, she was as sarcastic as she could be with people, who offended her, pleased her and did no harm. This aspect of the novel was one of those touches, which filled people with admiration for the writer.

After completing *Nicholas Nickleby,* Dickens resigned from his editorship of Bentley's Miscellany, in which *Oliver Twist* originally appeared. He conceived the idea of a weekly periodical to be issued as *Master Humphrey's Clock.* This was to comprise short stories, essays and

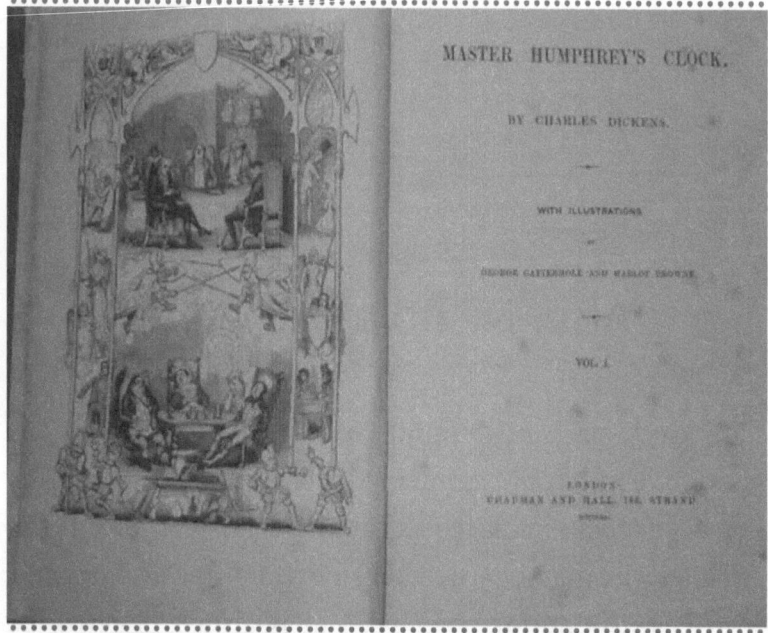

miscellaneous papers, after the model of Addison's Spectator.

Of the first number of the *Clock,* nearly seventy thousand were sold. But people concluded that there was no continuous tale. As a result, the orders at once diminished. There was an interval of three numbers between the first and second chapters, which the society of Mr Pickwick and the two Wellers made pleasant enough. But, after the introduction of Dick Swiveller, there were three consecutive chapters. In the continued progress of the tale to it's close, there were only two more breaks, one between the fourth and fifth chapters and one between the eighth and ninth. Dickens made the chapters pardonable and enjoyable by introducing Sam and his father. The re-introduction of those old favourites was a part of his original plan to make the magazine sell.

However, this time, the public demanded a story from Dickens. Thus, commenced *The Old Curiosity Shop*, which was continued with slight interruptions and followed by *Barnaby Rudge*. For the first time, Dickens was obsessed with a highly complicated plot. The tonality achieved in *The Old Curiosity Shop* surpassed anything he had attempted in this difficult vein. At the same time, the rich humour of Dick Swiveller and the Marchioness and the vivid portraiture of the wandering Bohemians attained the very highest level of Dickensian humour. However, in the lamentable tale of Little Nell, people, in general, admitted that he committed an indecent assault upon the

emotions. He exhibited an out-and-out monster of piety and longsuffering in a child of tender years. In *Barnaby Rudge*, he was manifestly affected by the influence of Scott, whose achievements he always regarded with a touching veneration. The plot again is of the utmost complexity and Edgar Allan Poe, who predicted the conclusion, must be one of the few persons who ever really mastered it. But few of Dickens' books are written in a more admirable style.

Chapter 16

Bleak House and Further Works

In 1851, Dickens started working on the somewhat dreary and jumbled *Bleak House*. In 1852, it started appearing as a monthly. However, September 1853 saw its last issue. Followed by this, Dickens wrote *Hard Times*, which was published in 1854. This novel had an anti-Manchester School tract, which Ruskin regarded as Dickens' best work. It was the first long story written for *Household Words*. About this time Dickens had made his final home at Gad's Hill, near Rochester. Along with that, he had put the finishing touch to another long novel, *Little Dorrit* (1855—1857).

In spite of the exquisite comedy of the master of the Marshalsea and the final tragedy of the central figure, Little Dorrit is sadly deficient in the old vitality and the humour appears like a mock reality. The repetition of comic catchwords and over-strung similes and metaphors is such as to cause nerve irritation in readers. The plot and characters ruin each other in this formless production.

The Tale of Two Cities commenced in All the Year Round, which was the successor of Household Words. The novel was resented before the readers in 1859 and was much better. The main characters are powerful. The story appears genuinely tragic and the atmosphere is lurid. But enormous labour was everywhere expended upon the construction of stylistic decoration of the plot.

Two finer efforts at atmospheric delineation followed *The Tale of Two Cities*. They are considered to be the best things Dickens ever did of this kind. He completed Great Expectations (1861) and *Our Mutual Friend* (1865).

Great Expectations began as a serialised publication in Dickens' periodical *All the Year Round* on December 1, 1860. The story of Pip (Philip Pirrip) was among Tolstoy's

and Dostoyevsky's favourite novels. Pip, an orphan, lives with his old sister and her husband. He meets an escaped convict named Abel Magwitch and helps him against his will. Magwitch is recaptured and Pip is taken care of by Miss Havisham. He falls in love with the cold-hearted Estella, Miss Havisham's ward. With the help of an anonymous benefactor, Pip is properly educated and he becomes a snob. Magwitch turns out to be the benefactor; he dies and Pip's 'great expectations' are ruined. He works as a clerk in a trading firm and marries Estella, Magwitch's daughter.

Chapter 17

A Second Visit to America

Our Mutual Friend was the second last novel Dickens wrote. It started with a murder mystery. In the opening chapter, a drowned man is found floating on the Thames. The Italian writer Italo Calvino has called the novel "an unqualified masterpiece, both in its plot and in the way it is written."

The general effect produced by the two novels, was, however, very, different.

In November 1867, Dickens made a second expedition to America, leaving all the writing that he was ever to complete behind him. He was to make a round sum of money, enough to free him from all embarrassments. He planned to make money by a long series of exhausting readings. He read with his fascinating style at the Tremont Temple, Boston, on December 2. The strain of Dickens' ordinary life was so tense and so continuous that it would be rash to assume that he broke down under this particular stress.

Dickens' persistence in these readings, subsequent to his return, was strongly criticised by his literary friends. It was a long testimony to Dickens' self-restraint, even in the most unpredictable and despotic moments of his career.

His farewell reading was given on March 15, 1870, at St. James's Hall. He then vanished from "those garish lights," as he called them, "forevermore." Of the three brief months that remained to him, his last book, *The Mystery of Edwin Drood,* occupied his entire attention. However, it hardly promised to become a masterpiece. It contained much fine descriptive technique, grouped round a scene of which Dickens had an unrivalled sympathetic knowledge.

The novel was published in 1870, but Dickens did not manage to finish it. He planned to produce it in 12 monthly

parts but managed to complete only six numbers. The story is chiefly set in the cathedral city of Cloisterham and opens in an opium den. The choirmaster of the cathedral, John Jaspers, lives a double life, as an opium addict and a respected member of society. His ward, Edwin Drood, disappears on Christmas Eve, after a quarrel with Neville Landless. However, there is no trace of Edwin's body. Dick Datchery, a disguised detective arrives to investigate the case.

Chapter 18

Dickens' Schedule and His Style

Dickens revelled in punctual and regular work. At his desk, he was often in the highest spirits. His writing was the only source of his pride and joy. The secret of such work as that of Dickens is that he did it with delight, in a sense easily. He wrote with the mechanism of mind and body in splendid order. In his later life, Dickens produced novels, which were though less excellent, but had much more of mental strain. The effects of age could not have shown themselves so soon, but unfortunately, he lost most of his energy in his non-literary labours.

To contemporaries, Dickens was not so much a man as an institution. At the very mention of his name, faces were puckered with grins or wreathed in smiles. To many, his work was a revelation. His literature revealed a new world and one far better than anyone has known.

Furthermore, Dickens' influence went further than anything else in the direction of revolution or revival. It gave what was then universally referred to as 'the lower

orders', a new sense of self-respect, a new feeling of citizenship. Like the defiance of another Luther or the Declaration of a new Independence, it emitted a fresh ray of hope across the sky. He did for the whole English-speaking race what Burns had done for Scotland. He gave the English speaking a new conceit of it. He knew what people wanted to know and be told what he knew.

Even though, true to his middle-class vein, Dickens praised goodness, chastity and honesty in a manner somewhat alien to the mind of the lowbred man. This is what makes Dickens such a demigod and his public success such a marvel. This also is why any exclusively literary' criticism of his work is bound to be so inadequate. The way he presented every truth, every detail, helps one to make the necessary allowances for the man-Dickens, even the Dickens of the legend that the world knows, is far from perfect.

Mr G. K. Chesterton once remarked suggestively that Dickens had all his life the faults of the little boy, who was kept up too late at night. He was overexcited by happiness to the verge of frustration. Yet, as a matter of fact, he did keep on the right side of the breaking point. The specific and curative work in his case was the work in which he took such anxious pride and such unmitigated delight.

Chapter 19
Final Years

On 9 June 1865, while returning from Paris with Ellen Ternan, Dickens was caught in the middle of the Staplehurst rail crash. The train's first seven carriages fell off a cast-iron bridge that was under repair. The only first-class carriage that had not met with the fatal crash was the one in which Dickens was travelling. Before help arrived, Dickens attended to and comforted the wounded and the dying with a flask of brandy and a hat refreshed with water, and saved some lives. Before leaving, he suddenly remembered the unfinished manuscript of *Our Mutual Friend*, and he quickly returned to his carriage to retrieve it.

Dickens later used this experience, his near-brush with death, as a basis and inspiration for his short ghost story, "*The Signal Man*", in which the central character suddenly sees an image of his own death in a rail crash. He also based the story on several previous rail accidents, such as the Clayton Tunnel rail crash of 1861. Dickens managed to avoid attending the inquest to prevent disclosing that he had been travelling with Ternan and her mother, something that would have certainly caused a scandal. After the crash, Dickens was often nervous while travelling by train, and would look for other alternative means of transport when available.

In 1868 he wrote, "I have sudden vague rushes of terror, even when riding in a hansom cab, which are perfectly unreasonable but quite insurmountable." Dickens's son, Henry, stated, "I have seen him sometimes in a railway carriage when there was a slight jolt. When this happened he was almost in a state of panic and gripped the seat with both hands."

In the early months of 1870, Dickens, as was his habit, started mixing with the best society. He dined with the prince at Lord Houghton's and twice attended court. On one occasion, he was at a private interview with the queen, something he had kept on the backseat for a long time. The Queen had given him a presentation copy of her leaves from a *Journal of our Life in the Highlands*. Dickens consistently refused to accept an honorary title given to him.

The Queen begged him to accept the nominal distinction of a privy councillor. He resided for four months, at Milner Gibsons' house at 5 Hyde Park Place, opposite the Marble Arch. There, he gave a brilliant reception on April 7. His last public appearance was at the Royal Academy, banquet early in May.

Dickens returned to his regular methodical routine of work at Gad's Hill on May 30, 1870.

There, he wrote one of the last instalments of *Edwin Drood*.

Dickens' health had started deteriorating in the 1860s. The fact that he had started doing public readings of his works in 1858 brought even greater a physical toll on him.

Chapter 20

Literary Style

Dickens's approach to the novel was influenced by various things, including the tradition of writing adventures of a rough and traditional hero, melodrama and the novel of sensibility. Perhaps the most important literary influence on him came from the fables of *The Arabian Nights*.

His writing style is marked by abundant linguistic creativity. Satire and his gift for caricature was his forte. An early reviewer compared him to Hogarth for his keen practical sense of the absurd side of life.

Dickens worked intensely on developing unique names for his characters that would grab the attention of all of his readers. It resonated with all of his artistic friends and associates. The names also indicated the theme and mood of the story- silly names were given to silly and dull characters, while serious names to intense and brooding ones. To cite one of the numerous examples, the name Mr Murdstone in *David Copperfield* conjures up twin references to "murder" and stony coldness in a reader's mind.

Dickens' literary style was also a mixture of fantasy and realism. His satires of British aristocratic arrogance—he calls one character the "Noble Refrigerator"—are often popular. Comparing orphans to stocks and shares, people to tug boats or dinner-party guests to furniture are just some of Dickens's celebrated flights of fancy.

The author worked closely with his illustrators, supplying them with a summary of the work at the beginning and thus made sure that his characters and settings were exactly how he imagined them. He would often brief the illustrator about plans for each month's instalment so that work could begin before he wrote them. Marcus Stone, the illustrator of *Our Mutual Friend*, recalled that the author was always "ready to describe down to the minutest details the personal characteristics, and ... life-history of the creations of his fancy".

Chapter 21

Characters

Often regarded as one of the greatest creators of characters in English fiction, next to none other than Shakespeare, Dickens's characters were some of the most memorable and loved. With beautiful and whimsical names such as Tiny Tim, Jacob Marley,Ebenezer Scrooge, Oliver Twist, The Artful Dodger, Fagin and Bill Sikes, Bob Cratchit (*A Christmas Carol*), David Copperfield, Uriah Heep and Mr Micawber (*David Copperfield*), Sam Weller(*The Pickwick Papers*) and Wackford Squeers (*Nicholas Nickleby*), his characters established themselves among the greatest characters in fiction, of all time, and have now become a part and parcel of popular culture. Some of them have also become a part of everyday language, *scrooge*, for example, means someone who is a miser or someone who dislikes spending money on Christmas festivities.

His characters were often so memorable that they became popular as household names outside his books. "Gamp" was slang for an umbrella, from the character Mrs Gamp, and "Pickwickian", "Pecksniffian", and "Gradgrind"

all entered dictionaries soon. Many were drawn from real life: Mrs Nickleby was based on his mother, though she didn't recognise herself in the story just as Mr Micawber was based on parts of his father's erratic behaviour.

Harold Skimpole in *Bleak House* was based on James Henry Leigh Hunt. Perhaps Dickens's meeting with Hans Christian Andersen made him create the character of the ugly and wicked Uriah Heep (now synonymous with sycophant).

Virginia Woolf wrote that "we remodel our psychological geography when we read Dickens" as he produces "characters who exist not in detail, not accurately or exactly, but abundantly in a cluster of wild yet extraordinarily revealing remarks".

T. S. Eliot wrote that Dickens "excelled in character; in the creation of characters of greater intensity than human beings."

London itself is one character that is repeatedly written about in Dickens' novels. Dickens described London as a beautiful magic lantern, that inspired the places and many people in his novels. From London's coaching inns, taverns, bars on the outskirts of the city to the lower banks of the Thames, all aspects of Dickens' London – are described throughout his body of work.

Chapter 22
Social Commentary

Dickens' best works mostly described society. He was a critic of the poverty and social classification in British society. In a New York address, he was famously quoted saying, "Virtue shows quite as well in rags and patches as she does in purple and fine linen". Dickens's second novel, *Oliver Twist* (1839), shocked readers with its descriptions of poverty and crime.

At a time when Britain was the major economic and political power of the world, Dickens wrote about the lives of the poor and downtrodden in society. Through his writings, he drove attention to specific issues—such as sanitation and the conditions in the workhouse—but his fiction probably showed its greatest powers by changing public opinion about class and social inequalities.

His writings often depicted the exploitation and oppression of the poor. He criticised the public officials and institutions that not only allowed such abuses to exist but were flourishing as a result. He most harshly criticised these conditions in his novel, *Hard Times* (1854), Dickens's sole novel-length treatment of the industrial working class. In this work, he uses anger and sarcasm to show how this marginalised social class was termed "hands" by the factory owners; that is, not really "people" but rather only parts of the machines they operated. His writings inspired others, in particular, journalists and political figures, to write about such problems of class oppression.

For example, the prison scenes in *The Pickwick Papers* led to the shutting down of the Fleet Prison. Karl Marx wrote how Dickens "issued to the world more political and social truths than have been uttered by all the professional politicians, publicists and moralists put together".George Bernard Shaw too remarked that *Great Expectations* was more rebellious than Karl Marx's *Das Kapital.*

Chapter 23

Reputation

Dickens was among the most popular novelists in his times and remains one of the best-known and most-loved of English authors. His works have never been out of print and have been adapted continually for the screen since the invention of cinema, with at least 200 films and TV adaptations based on his works made. A lot of his works were adapted for the stage and theatre in his own lifetime, and in 1913, *The Pickwick Papers*, a silent film based on the novel of the same name was made.

Some of the world's most beloved and popular fictional characters of the Victorian era were created by Dickens. However his fame turned into a downward spiral with the publication of *Bleak House*. Dark and honest in its descriptions, *Bleak House* wasn't liked by many, since it was very different in its tone than Dickens' usual writing. Book reviewers and literary figures in the 1850s, '60s and '70s, saw *Bleak House* as a decline from his bright, comic works to dark and serious reality. Despite these reviews and comments, the people never really grew to dislike

Dickens. Dickens's fame remained, sales continued to rise, and *Household Words* and *All the Year Round* were highly successful.

In the later stage of his career, Dickens' fame and the public demand for his readings were unmatched. *The Times* wrote in 1868 wrote about, how, amidst all the readings, those by Charles Dickens were second to none. Comparing his reception to a pop star, *The Guardian* wrote about how people sometimes fainted at his shows.

For 70 years after his death, Dickens received very little attention from the literary intelligentsia. Notable exceptions were George Gissing, G. K. Chesterton, John Cowper Powys and George Bernard Shaw.

The French writer, Jules Verne once called Dickens his favourite writer. The Dutch painter Vincent van Gogh was inspired by Dickens's novels and in many of his paintings, like *Vincent's Chair,* references to Dickens' work could be found. In an 1899 letter to his sister, Vincent wrote, that *A Christmas Carol* was one of the few things, that was keeping him from committing suicide. Virginia Woolf loved and hated his works equally, stating that while his novels were mesmerizing, his writing was too sentimental and was sometimes, ordinary.

Chapter 24

A Man of Outstanding Letters

Nowadays no one can think of writing letters like the ones written by Dickens. His elaborate style of writing was absolutely unmatched.

Once he was on a trip with his friends, in Cornwall. In one of his letters from there, he wrote, "Heavens! if you could have seen the necks of bottles, distracting in their immense variety of shape, peering out of the carriage pockets! If you could have witnessed the deep devotion of the post-boys, the maniac glee of the waiters! If you could have followed us into the earthy old churches we visited and into the strange caverns on the gloomy seashore and down into the depths of mines and up to the tops of giddy heights, where the unspeakably green water was roaring, I don't know how many hundred feet below. I never laughed in my life as I did on this journey. It would have done you good to hear me. I was choking and gasping and bursting the buckles off the back of my stock, all the way. And Stanfield -the painter- got into such apoplectic entanglements that we were obliged to beat him on the back with portmanteaus before we could recover him."

Bob Fagin was one of Dickens' closest friends in the warehouse. Years later, in a letter to his friend, he wrote about the day in the warehouse, when he was suffering from illness, "Bob Fagin was very good to me on the occasion of a bad attack of my old disorder. I suffered such excruciating pain that time, that they made a temporary bed of straw in my old recess in the counting-house and I rolled about on the floor and Bob filled empty blacking-bottles with hot water and applied relays of them to my side, half the day. I got better and quite easy towards evening, but Bob (who was much bigger and older than I) did not like the idea of my going home alone and took me under his protection. I was too proud to let him know about the prison; and after making several efforts to get rid of him, to all of which Bob Fagin in his goodness was deaf, shook hands with him on the steps of a house near Southwark-bridge on the Surrey side, making believe that I lived there. As a finishing piece of reality in case of his looking back, I knocked at the door, I recollect and asked, when the woman opened it if that was Mr Robert Fagin's house."

In another letter his friend, Dickens wrote,

"My Dear Collins,— I hope you are as well as I am and have as completely shaken off all your ailings. And I hope, too, that you are disposed of for a long visit here. We are established in a doll's country house of many rooms in a delightful garden. If you have anything to do, this is the place to do it in. And if you have nothing to do, this is also the place to do it into perfection. You shall have a Pavilion room in the garden, with a delicious view, where you may write no end of Basils. You shall get up your Italian as I raise the fallen fortunes (at present sorely depressed) of mine. You shall live, with a delicate English graft upon the best French manner and learn to get up early in the morning again. In short, you shall be thoroughly prepared, during the whole summer season, for those great travels that are to come off anon.

Do turn your thoughts this way, coming by South Eastern *Tidal Train* (there is a separate list for that train, the time changing every day as the tide varies), you come in five hours. No passport wanted. Mrs Dickens and her sister send their kind regards and beg me to say how glad they will be to see you."

Chapter 25
A Chronology of Dickens' Life

1812

Born on Friday, 7 February at Landport, a suburb of Portsmouth to John, a clerk in the navy pay-office attached to the dockyard and Elizabeth Dickens.

1814

Father transferred to London with family.

1816

Father transferred to Chatham with family. First gets some schooling, although already an avid reader.

1824

Father arrested for debt on February 2 and consigned to the Marshalsea, where the family joins him. Separated from family and put to work at Warren's Blacking Factory at Hungerford Market. Eventually family finds him some lodging in Lant Street close to them. After father's release on May 28, the family returns to Camden Town. Charles attends day school in Hampstead Road, London.

1827

Taken from school. Becomes office boy of an attorney; decides to become a journalist.

1829

Freelance reporter at Doctor's Commons Courts.

1831

Acts as a parliamentary reporter during the Reform Bill agitation.

1834

While working as a newspaper reporter, Charles adopts the pseudonym "Boz." Father once again arrested for debt; Charles comes to his aid.

1835

Becomes engaged to Catherine Hogarth, daughter of his friend George Hogarth, an editor.

1836

His first series of *Sketches by Boz* published; receives 150 pounds for the copyright.

The first instalment of *Pickwick Papers* appears on March 30.

Marries Catherine Hogarth on April 2.

Becomes an editor of *Bentley's Miscellany*. Publishes in December the second series of *Sketches by Boz*.

1837

Begins *Oliver Twist*; continues in monthly parts in *Bentley's Miscellany*.

Catherine's younger sister Mary, whom he idolises, dies.

Catherine bears a son Charles, the first of seven sons and three daughters.

Pickwick Papers finishes.

1838

Begins writing *Nicholas Nickleby*

1839

Resigns as editor of *Bentley's Miscellany*. Last part of *Oliver Twist* appears in April. *Nicholas Nickleby* finishes in October.

1840

The first instalment of *Master Humphrey's Clock*, which becomes his next two stories, appears. Begins *The Old Curiosity Shop*.

1841

Finishes The Old Curiosity Shop in February. Begins *Barnaby Rudge*, which continues through November.

1842

Travels through Canada and the United States. *American Notes* appears in October.

1844

Tours Italy with family. Returns to London in December, when *The Chimes* is published. Leaves London for Genoa.

1849

David Copperfield begins running.

1850

David Copperfield finishes in November. Founds and edits the weekly Household Words.

1851

Begins work on *Bleak House.*

1852

Bleak House begins to appear monthly.

1853

Bleak House ends in September. Tours Italy with Augustus Egg and Wilkie Collins. Returns to England. Gives the first of many public readings from his own works. Summers in Boulogne.

1854

Hard Times appears weekly in Household Words until August. Spends the summer with his family and fall in Boulogne.

1855

Little Dorrit begins to appear monthly.

1857

Little Dorrit ends in June. With family spends summer at renovated Gad's Hill.

1858

In London, undertakes his first public readings for pay. Quarrels with Thackeray. Separates from Catherine.

1859

His London readings continue. Begins new weekly, *All the Year Round*. *A Tale of Two Cities* appears, continues through November.

1860

His family takes up residence at Gad's Hill. Burns many personal letters. *Great Expectations* begins to appear weekly.

1861

Embarks on yet another series of public readings in London. *Great Expectations* finishes in August.

1862

His public readings continue.

1863

Continues public readings in Paris and London. Reconciles with Thackeray just before the latter's death.

1864

Our Mutual Friend begins to appear monthly. Health begins to fail, much because of overwork.

1865

Railway accident badly shakes him and Ellen Ternan. *Our Mutual Friend* ends in November.

1867

Continues public readings in England and Ireland. Unwell but carries on, against doctor's advice. Embarks on an American reading tour.

1868

Finishes his American reading tour. His health worsens but takes additional duties at *All the Year Round.*

1869

Continues readings in England, Scotland and Ireland. Shows symptoms of mild stroke; provincial readings cancelled. Begins *The Mystery of Edwin Drood.*

1870

Dies on June 9 and is buried at Westminster Abbey on June 14. Last of his unfinished *Mystery of Edwin Drood* appears in September.